THE AMAZING SPIDER-MAN

MARVEL

VS M

Based on the Marvel comic book series Spider-Man
Adapted by **Michael Siglain**
Illustrated by **Todd Nauck** *and* **Hi-Fi Design**

Published by Marvel Press, an
imprint of Disney Book Group.
No part of this book may be
reproduced or transmitted in
any form or by any means,
electronic or mechanical, including
photocopying, recording, or by any
information storage and retrieval
system, without written permission
from the publisher.

For information address Marvel
Press, 114 Fifth Avenue, New York,
New York 10011-5690.
Printed in the United States of
America
First Edition
1 3 5 7 9 10 8 6 4 2
G658-7729-4-12214
ISBN 978-1-4231-5424-2

marvelkids.com

New York

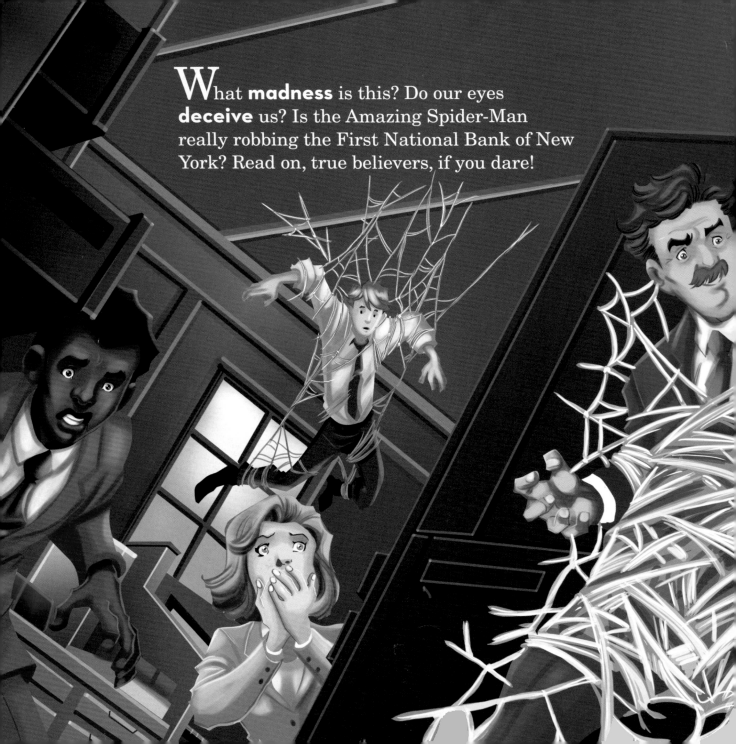

What **madness** is this? Do our eyes **deceive** us? Is the Amazing Spider-Man really robbing the First National Bank of New York? Read on, true believers, if you dare!

Having robbed the bank, the now-**sinister** Spider-Man escapes by crawling up the side of the building!

Not even New York's Finest can catch the
web-slinger in time. Spider-Man is no longer a
hero, but a **wanted criminal!**

At Midtown High, student Peter Parker and his friends are surprised to learn of Spider-Man's criminal caper.

If only Peter's friends knew that he was really Spider-Man! Peter knows that **he** did not rob that bank, so it must have been an **imposter!**

Peter can find out more at **The Daily Bugle,** and the fastest way to get there is as the Amazing Spider-Man!

At the **Bugle,** Peter speaks to his boss, J. Jonah Jameson, who has always believed that Spider-Man is a **menace.**

"Parker!" JJJ yells. "I need you to get a picture of Spider-Man breaking the law for the front page!"

Just then, a strange caped figure appears in Jonah's
office! He calls himself **Mysterio.** He tells JJJ that if
Spider-Man wants to learn the **truth,** he will meet the
web-slinger tomorrow morning atop the Brooklyn Bridge.

Spider-Man expects a **trap** but confronts Mysterio anyway. Mysterio tells Spider-Man that he will defeat the wall-crawler once and for all!

Mysterio's strange powers and abilities are too much for even Spider-Man!

With a wave of his hand, Mysterio **disintegrates** Spider-Man's webs right before Spidey's eyes!

Spider-Man lunges forward, but the menacing Mysterio
disappears into thin air!

Defeated, Peter returns to **The Daily Bugle.** But he can't believe his eyes—Mysterio is shaking hands with Jonah!

JJJ is happy to hear about Mysterio's fight with Spider-Man. He doesn't trust Spidey, and believes Mysterio to be New York's true hero.

Just as Mysterio is about to leave, Peter secretly places a small **homing device** on his cape.

Then, as Spider-Man, Peter uses the homing device to trace Mysterio to his **secret lair!**

Within minutes, Spider-Man tracks Mysterio to a television studio in Queens, New York, and startles the villain with his spider-signal.

Inside the television
studio, **Mysterio attacks!**

Spider-Man is down but not out. But Peter still needs to
know if Mysterio was the imposter who robbed the bank.
"Of course it was me." Mysterio cackles. "Who else would
have the **genius** to improve upon your powers?"

"Once I was a great special effects and makeup artist. But then the movies **changed,** and effects were done on computers. No one needed classic special effects anymore . . ."

". . . so I used **my skills** to duplicate **yours.** I created an entirely new character—the menacing Mysterio! And as Mysterio, I will defeat Spider-Man and become **the greatest hero** the world has ever known!

"For I am both the **criminal** and the **conqueror,** Spider-Man. Now prepare to meet your **doom!**"

Before Mysterio can strike again,
Spider-Man leaps into **action!**
But Mysterio knows the television
studio and knows exactly how to **escape!**

Mysterio runs through the set of
a science-fiction show, but he cannot
outrun the Amazing Spider-Man!

And so, with all of his super-strength, Spider-Man crashes down on Mysterio, knocking the villain out cold!

After turning Mysterio over to the police, Spidey calls on J. Jonah Jameson to let him know who the **real hero** is!

Later, Peter returns to Midtown High. He is relieved to find out that his friends believe Spider-Man is a hero again.

And so, the menacing Mysterio—with his maniacal movie magic—has been defeated by the **spectacular Spider-Man!**

THE CONTINENTAL

MIDNIGHT MONSTER FEST!
FEATURING
BEAST FROM BEYOND!
THE EYES OF STELLA!
DRACULA VS. MINA!